AMISH CARETAKER

Amish Romance

HANNAH MILLER

Tica House
Publishing

Sweet Romance that Delights and Enchants!

Personal Word from the Author

To My Dear Readers,

How exciting that you have chosen one of my books to read. Thank you! I am proud to now be part of the team of writers at Tica House Publishing who work joyfully to bring you stories of hope, faith, courage, and love.

Please feel free to contact me as I love to hear from my readers. I would like to personally invite you to sign up for updates and to become part of our **Exclusive Reader Club** —it's completely Free to join! Hope to see you there!

With love,

Hannah Miller

VISIT HERE to Join our Reader's Club and to Receive Tica House Updates:

https://amish.subscribemenow.com/

Chapter One

Norma Glick tried her best to suppress a feeling of quiet pride as she set the tin of shoofly pie down beside the other desserts that members of her community had laid out on the long tables in the Fisher barn. The delicious scent of the molasses-flavored treat was as sweet as it was simple, although Norma knew the amount of labor involved in making it because it was not only her handiwork, but also her own recipe. She stepped back, admiring her pie even though she knew she shouldn't be prideful.

"Mmm." Her youngest brother, Ruben, butted into her reverie. "That smells so *gut*."

"Shoo, Ruben!" Norma laughed. "It's not just for you. Besides, you tasted the filling while I was making it."

"*Jah*, go away, Ruben," boomed a sturdy voice, and Norma's oldest brother playfully shoved Ruben aside. Abel winked at her, his eyes twinkling, and reached toward the pie dish. "This pie is too *gut* for the likes of you."

"Hey!" said Ruben, indignantly. "That's not true."

"This pie is meant to be savored." Abel leaned over it and took a long sniff. "Not just gulped down the way you eat, *brudder*."

Norma slapped Abel's hands away and brandished a dishcloth at all three of her brothers. "I'm warning you, I'll never bake for you again if you keep on like this."

Even though they knew this was an empty threat, Norma's brothers – Ruben, Abel, and the middle brother, Thaddeus – gave her a big-eyed look. Norma laughed. Ruben was the youngest at seventeen, but they all looked like naughty schoolboys.

"You'll have your share when everyone has settled down to the meal," she said.

Ruben's attention had already made its way to the other side of the throng of Amish people making their way out of the Fisher house, where the church service had been held in their meeting room, and toward the barn for the post-service meal. Thaddeus gave his brother a playful elbow.

"Who do you see, Ruben?" he asked.

Ruben turned scarlet. "No one," he said.

Thaddeus laughed, grabbing his brother's arm. "Come on – let's go and talk to her. I mean, let's go and talk to *no one*."

"*Nee*," protested Ruben, but it was no good. Thaddeus was towing him determinedly through the crowd, and Norma could only laugh and shake her head. She turned to Abel. "Where's Beulah today?"

"*Ach*, she's not well," he said, looking a little crestfallen. "She had to stay at home." He must have seen in her eyes the fear that gripped Norma's heart, for he reached out, putting a gentle hand on her shoulder. "She just ate something that didn't agree with her, Norma," he said. "Her *mudder* says she'll be just fine. Don't look so frightened."

Norma took a steadying breath. "I'm sorry. I know I shouldn't always think the worst when someone is ill, but ever since the influenza that..." She couldn't finish the sentence.

Abel gave her shoulder a reassuring squeeze. "None of us expected something like the flu to take our *mudder* from us, Norma. But you must remember she had a bad chest, just like her *mudder* before her. It was just too much for her."

Norma was suddenly blinded by tears. She nodded, wiping at them. "It's been so many years, but I still miss her," she whispered. "I wish I could just tell her all the little things, you know. About the thrush I saw in the garden this morning when I was getting breakfast ready." She sniffed, half laughing. "Even about my own shoofly pie recipe."

"She would have loved your pie. You got your baking skills from her."

"*Danke*, Abel. You're *gut* at making me feel better," she said, smiling.

"And you're *gut* at appreciating and caring for people." A note of sorrow crept into Abel's eyes. "Just like she was."

"I'm going to need to be *gut* at caring for people over the next few weeks." Norma groaned. "It sounds like *Onkel* Silas is going to be something of a handful."

Abel let out a groan of his own. "Don't remind me," he said. "I was fine with seeing the grumpy old toad only once a year."

"Abel! Don't call him a toad." Norma swatted at him with the dishcloth.

"He looks like a toad," said Abel. "And he just sits there croaking at you all the time."

Norma held back a laugh, then she shook her head solemnly. "Don't speak like that of your elders, *brudder*. Besides, you sound like a schoolboy. You're twenty-one, you know."

"I'm not looking forward to Silas coming to stay," said Abel. "Especially since he can't take care of himself right now. He's going to be more demanding than ever."

"It's only going to be for a few weeks," said Norma sensibly. "Besides, he won't be so bad. You'll see. And even if he *is* bad, *Gott* expects us to treat him with love and kindness."

"You're right, as usual." He gave her arm a squeeze. "The men are all sitting down to the meal — I suppose I'd better join them."

Norma patted her brother's back. "Off you go then, *brudder*."

Norma watched Abel join the crowd of men that was settling down on the long wooden benches. The barn was a little stuffy, but its familiar scent, laced with the delicious smells of an Amish meal, was home to Norma. Sunlight slanted in through the small, high windows, peppered with golden motes of dust. She watched them dance, realizing how happy she should be here at this merry gathering with the family she adored. But there was a gentle emptiness in her heart, a longing that she couldn't quite drown out no matter how hard she worked.

That longing was for a young man with pitch-black hair who had just dished up his first helping and was looking for a spot where he could sit down. His rowdy friends called out to him, holding up their hands, but the young man's piercing green eyes had settled on a newcomer to the community sitting off to one side. He waved merrily to his friends and then headed over to the open space, sparking a smile from the newcomer as he sat down.

"You shouldn't stare so hard, you know," a voice whispered by Norma's shoulder. "You'll burn a hole in his shirt."

Norma turned, feeling her cheeks heating. "I-I wasn't staring," she said.

Her best friend, Dinah, gave a teasing giggle. Her brown eyes twinkled with kindness underneath her *kapp*. "Not at all," she said. "Neither is the sky blue, or summer hot, or the grass green, or—"

"All right, all right," Norma hissed. "But don't talk about it." She raised her hands to her hot cheeks.

"Why not?" said Dinah. "It's perfectly understandable for you to be sweet on Trevor Schwartz. He's a *gut* man, kind and generous, and he'll inherit a beautiful farm one day." She smiled. "If I wasn't already being courted by Joel, I might be looking at Trevor just the same way that you are."

"He is rather *wunderlich*," said Norma wistfully.

"So why do you avoid him anytime there's a gathering?" asked Dinah. "I've only seen you two speak three or four times. You can't ask him to court you, of course, but maybe you could give him the chance to know you a little better."

"It's not that simple."

"Why not?" Dinah put her head to one side, her eyes filling with sympathy. "Is it because of all the work you have to do to help your family?"

"*Nee...* not this time," said Norma.

"Ever since your *Mamm* died, you've been working awful hard to care for your *daed* and all four siblings," said Diane gently. She laid a hand on Norma's back. "It can't be easy to be courting at the same time."

"It wouldn't be," Norma admitted. "That's why I've never had a beau before. That's why sometimes..." She trailed off, not wanting to say the words out loud because of their ungrateful flavor. *That's why sometimes I think I'll never be able to have a family of my own.* She shook her head. "But it's something else this time."

"What, then?" asked Dinah.

Norma nodded towards where Trevor was still sitting. "That."

Dinah looked over. A beautiful young woman – tall and shapely in all the ways that Norma was short and plain – walked past the table, bearing a glass of fruit punch. She paused when Trevor held out a hand to her, and he smiled up at her, a happy, secret expression that nobody would have noticed except if they were watching closely—and Norma was watching very, very closely.

"Oh," said Dinah. "Really? Prissy Raber?"

"*Jah.*" Norma sighed. "I'm sure they're courting."

Dinah shook her head, patting Norma's arm. "Prissy is a *gut maidel*, but they're not married yet," she said encouragingly. "Maybe one day, Trevor will love you after all."

"Maybe one day," Norma echoed wistfully. But she knew that it was about as likely as the deacons allowing her to drive a car.

Chapter Two

"*Ach,* Sheba!" Norma lamented, looking up from the table she was scrubbing as her younger sister ran past the kitchen door. "Where are your shoes?"

Caught in the act of running down the hallway in her socks, Sheba skidded to a halt. She crept into the room, looking up at Norma from underneath her pale golden lashes. "Um..." she began.

"And look at your dress. It's filthy!" said Norma, annoyed. "Have you been playing with the horses again this morning?"

"Pepper needed the exercise," Sheba protested. "I couldn't just leave him in the field all day."

"Sheba." Norma groaned. "*Daed* will be here with Onkel Silas any minute, and I've been running around the *haus* all morning to get everything looking *gut*. Now, you look like an orphan." She angrily pointed upstairs. "Go and get changed!"

"You're not *Mamm*, you know," said Sheba.

"*Nee*, I'm your older *shvestah*, and if you don't get changed right now, I'll get *Daed* to ground you from tending the horses *and* make you clean the chicken coop," said Norma threateningly. "Now go!"

Sheba stuck out her tongue, but nonetheless ran upstairs, and Norma let out a sigh. Her little sister was about to turn thirteen, and Norma wondered if she'd ever been as annoying as a teenager. Probably not – she'd still been in eighth grade when *Mamm* had died. That had forced her to grow up fast.

Finishing with the table, she paused to peer into the oven. The casserole she was making smelled good – it would be ready in a few minutes. She bustled across the passage from the kitchen into the sewing room that she and her brothers had converted into a bedroom, since Silas couldn't climb stairs anymore. It had saddened her to rake up all of *Mamm*'s things and stuff them into cupboards, but at least the room looked tidy. A bed was pushed up into the corner; there was an empty wardrobe waiting for Silas's clothes, and the wooden floor was so clean and shiny that Norma could nearly see her face in it.

Footsteps sounded on the stairs, and Norma hurried out of the room. "Ruben!" she hollered.

"What?" Ruben shouted from the landing.

"Are you changed into clean clothes yet?"

"Am I supposed to change into clean clothes?"

"*Jah*, Ruben," Norma bellowed. She turned, almost bumping into another of her brothers, and grabbed his arm. "You too, Thaddeus. Off you go. We're going to make Silas feel welcome."

"Can't I make him feel welcome in this shirt?" asked Thaddeus.

"It has cow manure on it," said Norma.

"So?"

"Just get changed, Thaddeus," Norma ordered. "I'm going to sweep off the porch."

She was still working her broom across the wood when Abel came strolling out of the house, holding a glass of lemonade and smelling strongly of sawdust. Norma put the broom down and glared at him.

"What?" said Abel.

"You, too? Really, Abel?" said Norma.

Abel looked down at his greasy shirt. "I was thirsty," he protested.

A buggy rumbled in the lane, and Norma looked up. She could

just catch a glimpse of the high black top of the buggy and a pair of bay ears traveling towards them over the hedge that lined their property. "Oh, never mind," she said, giving up. "They're here. Please call Ruben, Thaddeus and Sheba for me?"

Abel opened the front door and yelled into the house at the top of his lungs. "EVERYONE! THEY'RE HERE!"

Norma shook her head. She hurried into the kitchen, almost getting run over by the stampede of her younger siblings and stashed the broom in a corner. Quickly running her eye over what she could see of the house, Norma breathed a sigh of relief. Nothing was out of place, except for Abel's shirt. Her home looked as clean and tidy as if an army of people had spent the morning on it, not just her. Silas would feel welcome – and that he was going to be well cared for.

When she made her way back outside, the buggy had come to a halt in the yard, and Thaddeus was holding the horse while *Daed* climbed out. He paused at the bottom of the two steps up into the buggy and held out a hand, his eyes concerned. "Are you all right there, *brudder*?"

Silas was about to emerge. Norma squared her shoulders, putting on her best and most hospitable smile.

"Silas?" *Daed* prompted.

An old man appeared hunched over in the doorway of the buggy, and Norma's first thought was that Abel's description of him as a toad was as accurate as it was unkind. The old man had a sagged, squashed appearance, as if he had once been just as tall and broad-shouldered as *Daed*, but the passage of the years had dragged everything downward – the folds of his portly figure, the bags underneath his eyes, and even the corners of his wide mouth. His eyes were deeply black and glittering, and they raked Norma and her siblings with a steady glare.

"All right?" he spluttered, puffing as he began to negotiate the steps down, ignoring *Daed*'s outstretched hand. "How could I be all right? Hours and hours it's been in this buggy to Indiana, and you did your best to drive that half-dead nag of yours over every single rock and bump in the road. Almost broke every bone in my body, you did. It's a mercy that—"

The torrent of anger paused for a minute when Silas stepped down from the last step. He staggered, his knees almost buckling, and *Daed* lunged to grab his arm. Norma saw the color draining from Silas's face, and she felt a pang of surprise. Now that she was looking more closely, she could see gray lines peppering his hair and long beard. It seemed as though he had aged a decade in the year since she'd last seen him.

"Silas? What's the matter?" *Daed* asked.

Silas straightened, shaking *Daed*'s arm off. "What's the matter? The fuss you've all been making, that's what," he sputtered. "All of you *shvestahs* and *brudders* of mine have been on my back about coming to stay here even though I was perfectly fine right where I was."

"We were worried about you, Silas," said *Daed* patiently.

"Was that any reason to kidnap me from my own home and drag me here to this..." Silas looked up at the house. Norma felt her stomach clench. The old man shook his head. "I don't have words for this, Amos. Last time I was here, Naomi was still alive. She would be ashamed of the state of things around here."

His words were like a punch in the mouth. Norma saw *Daed* look at her, saw apology flit across his face, but she still felt as though she'd been stabbed. Tears prickled at her eyes, but she blinked them back and pasted a smile onto her face. She had promised herself that she would be kind to Silas.

She would make herself do it – for just a few weeks.

Norma spooned stew out of the pot in a series of sharp movements, slapping it down onto the pile of mashed potatoes on the center of the plate so hard that sauce splattered in all directions. She planted the plate down on the middle of the table with a clank, then began to rummage around in the cutlery drawer, shoving knives and forks aside as she dug for the special cutlery with which Silas would deign to eat. Throwing the knife and fork down on the table, she grabbed a glass from the kitchen cupboard and slammed it onto the counter.

"Easy, *shvestah*," said Abel's voice from the doorway. "What's that glass ever done to you?"

Norma turned to glare at her brother. He leaned against the doorframe, his arms crossed, his eyes mildly amused. "Nothing," she snapped at him. "Where's everyone else? I told you lunch was ready ten minutes ago!"

"Slow down there." Abel's smile was good-natured as he held up his hands. "It wasn't me, I promise."

Norma let out a slow sigh. Abel was right – he'd done nothing wrong. "Sorry, *brudder*," she said. "I'm not mad at you."

"Are you mad at the cutlery and crockery, then?" said Abel, raising an eyebrow. "Because the way you were throwing it around, it definitely looked like it."

"*Nee*. It's…" Norma groaned, flopping down in a kitchen chair and buried her face in her hands. Frustration welled up in her like an angry growth.

Abel pulled out a chair beside her and sat down, laying a hand on her shoulder. "Let me guess. Is it a certain grouchy old man who's done this to my sweet, gentle sister?"

"*Jah!*" Norma almost shouted the word. She took another deep breath and held it for a moment, trying to calm herself. "I've never had anyone make me so angry before,

Abel. Ever since Silas has been here, life just hasn't been the same."

From upstairs, Norma could hear Sheba singing to herself as she washed her hands. She rubbed her temples. "I know my duty is to serve," she said, "but Silas treats me like a slave."

"He's not been particularly kind to any of us," said Abel. "He made Sheba cry last night when he told her that her dress looked like a flour sack."

"And I heard him telling Ruben he's so skinny because he's lazy and never does anything to build muscles," said Norma. "It seems like he's been bent on criticizing everything he sees ever since he first set foot in this *haus*. He even keeps telling *Daed* how he should run the farm or change the *haus*. He told me that the potatoes I gave him last night were raw. He says that I'm trying to poison him." Norma threw up her hands. "I don't know what to do with him."

"I know how you feel," said Abel. "I think it's…"

"YOU! *MAIDEL!*" Silas bellowed from the sewing room. "SHUT UP!"

Above them, Sheba's singing abruptly stopped.

"I can barely hear myself think with your racket!" Silas roared. "Don't you know how to behave?"

There was a sob from upstairs, and then running feet. Norma

groaned, leaning her forehead on the table. "He's made Sheba cry again."

"*Ach, shvestah*, it'll be all right," said Abel encouragingly, putting an arm around her shoulders. "You're just unhappy right now because you haven't baked in a week."

"I have time for nothing. I'm forever running around after Silas," moaned Norma.

"Don't worry. It's only for a few more weeks," said Abel. He gave her an affectionate squeeze. "I'll go and talk to Sheba and make her laugh. You do whatever it is that you're doing with that plate of food that has you so angry."

"Taking it to Silas," grumbled Norma. "He won't even come to the table for meals. It's so disrespectful!"

Abel moved out of the room, and Norma picked up the plate. She paused to wipe the splatters of sauce clean around the edges, knowing that Silas expected nothing less than perfection when it came to his food; she tried to gather some strength. Squaring her shoulders, she walked toward the sewing room. *Gott expects us to be kind to everyone,* she coached herself. *Even crotchety old toads.*

The door was closed, which was not unusual. Silas said the sounds of everyone walking up and down the hallway gave him a headache. Norma reached up and tapped softly on the door. "Onkel Silas?" she said. "Lunch is ready."

"Go away," Silas yelped.

Norma frowned. She would gladly have complied, but his voice sounded very different from the full-throated bellow he'd given Sheba just now.

"Are you all right?" she asked, leaning a little closer to the door.

"I told you to go away." There was definitely something wrong. Silas's voice was tearful and shaky. Broken.

"What's wrong?" Norma called softly. "Do you need help?"

There was a long, long pause. Just as Norma was about to ask again, a quiet voice whispered from within the room.

"*Jah.*"

His tone scared her. Norma opened the door and stepped inside. Silas was sitting on the edge of his bed, his pants around his ankles, his white underwear showing, and tears streaming down his cheeks. When he looked up at her, his mouth was twisted with bitter humiliation. A pungent odor filled the room, and Norma spotted a black stain spreading through Silas's underwear down his legs.

She stared at him. Revulsion and compassion clanged in her heart, and Silas looked away, a tear dripping down his cheek.

"I couldn't get to the bathroom in time," he said in a small voice, like a little boy caught in a naughty act.

The voice was what changed her heart. She put the plate down on the nightstand and walked over to him. "It's all right,

Onkel Silas," she said. "I'll help you. Don't worry. These little accidents happen."

Silas nodded mutely, and Norma went into the bathroom next door to his room to get a basin of hot water. Despite the smell hanging in the air, Norma's heart was filled with something new: compassion.

Silas was sicker than she'd thought.

Chapter Three

Norma gazed at the rows of bags of sugar on the shelves, staring from one price tag to the next, willing her tired eyes to read the numbers. Was the two-pound bag cheaper or more expensive per pound than the half-pound one? She pinched the bridge of her nose, willing her brain to work.

"Take this one," said a cheerful voice at her elbow. A hand reached around her, grabbing the two-pound bag and dumping it into the basket on her arm. "It's better value for money."

"Hello, Dinah." Norma smiled, a ripple of joy running through her at the sight of her friend.

"Hello, stranger." Dinah grinned, putting an arm around Norma's shoulders and leading her down the aisle of the

Amish market where they both loved to shop for groceries. "I haven't seen you since preaching Sunday."

"I know. Sorry," said Norma.

"You look exhausted," said Dinah. "What's the matter?"

Norma studied her friend for a moment. Dinah had never looked so happy. Her cheeks were glowing pink, her eyes so bright that she could almost see the sparkles in them. As they walked, she gave a little extra bounce with each stride, as if she were so filled with buoyant joy she might just float away and disappear. For the sake of Dinah's mood, Norma forced a grin. "Just a long night, that's all," she said, not wanting to tell Dinah that she'd been woken at midnight to help Silas to the bathroom. "You look like you've got something to tell me."

"I do," Dinah almost squealed. She spun in a little circle, making her apron rise in the air, and clapped her hands underneath her chin. "Oh, Norma, Joel and I are engaged!"

The news broke over Norma like a wave: breathtakingly cold. She stared at Dinah, at the light in her eyes, the grin that split her face in half, and she couldn't help it. Norma burst into tears.

"Norma!" Dinah rushed to grab her friend's hands. "What on earth is the matter?"

"*Ach*, Dinah, I'm sorry." Norma wrapped her arms around the girl, hugging her tightly. "I'm so happy for you. I truly am."

"Then why are you crying?" asked Dinah, her eyes filled with concern as she stepped back.

"I – I'm not jealous," said Norma, wiping her eyes with her apron. "I just – I want to feel what you're feeling, too." She swallowed hard. "And I don't think I ever will. I'll never get to court a young man. I'll never get married."

"Norma, my *liebchen*, what would give you that right foolish idea?" demanded Dinah.

"It's Silas," Norma wailed. "He's taken up every single scrap of my spare time – and I didn't have much. I can't go to the sings, or stay and talk to Trevor after church, or even come to see you because all I do is care for Silas. Even when we go to a gathering..." She stopped, taking a deep breath. "I'm so sorry, Dinah. I shouldn't complain. He's an old, sick man, and I'm honored to serve and care for him as Jesus would have. I'm just really, really tired."

"I can see that," said Dinah. She sighed, resting a hand on Norma's arm. "You haven't had an easy time of it ever since your *mudder* died."

Norma swallowed hard, wiping at her eyes again. "I miss her so much, Dinah," she said. "With my whole entire heart. I wish she was here just to give me some advice or to hold my hand when things get so hard."

"I can only imagine." Dinah gave her a hug. "It's hard now, I know. But trust in *Gott*'s will, my beloved friend. He has a *gut* plan for you, and even in this trial, He has something to teach you."

"*Danke,* Dinah," said Norma. "And congratulations. Really." She scraped together a smile. "You and Joel are going to be very happy together."

I just wish I could have that happiness too, one day, she added silently.

Norma's hands felt so empty. She sat still on the driver's seat of the buggy, squashed up between Sheba and her father. Silas wouldn't let Sheba sit in the back with him because she was too noisy, even though right now the little girl sat motionless, not uttering a single peep. Norma knew she was miserable, but for the moment, she was struggling to escape from her own misery as she gazed down into her empty lap. Ever since she could remember, she'd always had something in her hands as they drove to church, even if it was just a warm fresh loaf of friendship bread. But not today.

Today, Norma's lap was light, but her heart was heavy as she gazed down into her empty hands, barely listening to the merry clip-clop of the horse's hooves on the road. In the back of the buggy, she could hear Silas muttering grumpily – no doubt complaining about something to her brothers. She almost felt sorry for them stuck in the back there with him.

"Here we are." *Daed* sounded relieved as he brought the buggy to a halt outside the King family's home.

Norma felt her stomach pitch with worry. The King's driveway was filled with unhitched buggies, all the community's horses grazing in a nearby field. Everyone was assembled inside already. She half shoved Sheba down from the driver's seat. "Come on, Sheba," she said. "We're late."

"That's an understatement!" snorted Silas, being helped down out of the buggy by Thaddeus and Abel. "Everyone must be hearing the sermon already. Really, Amos, how you can dream of arriving at church this late is absolutely ridiculous. It's shameful, *brudder*. You're doing the Glick family name no *gut!*"

Norma felt a stirring of resentment in her stomach and tried to quell it. *He's just a sick old man,* she told herself. *And this is just for a few more weeks.* "Come on, *Onkel*," she said, holding out her hand. "Let me help you."

"You?" Silas snorted. "You must go and sit in the female section with the rest of the women." His eyes narrowed. "Don't you know that? Don't you bring them to church, Amos?"

Norma took a steadying breath. She'd meant that she could help Silas to the door, but clearly, he wasn't interested. He clung to Abel's arm instead as they headed toward the service, Silas's angry tirade flowing unabated. "You are going to have to do something about these *kinner* of yours, Amos," he was saying. "I've never seen something so terrible. Too lazy to be ready in time to get to preaching service, and now we're late. I've never been so ashamed in my life."

When Ruben eased the barn door open a crack, Norma realized that she had never been so embarrassed in her life. The intrusion on the quiet preaching was so unheard-of that the bishop actually stopped talking. Standing at the front of the barn, which was lined with hard wooden benches, the bishop leveled a stern glare at her and her family. Norma wished the earth would swallow her whole. She wished it would swallow Silas whole: it had been his continual fussing that had made her and her family late in the first place.

The bishop seemed to glower at her for an age before finally continuing with the sermon. The community quickly looked toward him, but she knew that for all the stiff necks in those long rows, every eye was following her as she grabbed Sheba's hand and hurried toward the nearest seat at the very back of the female section. She wanted to scream, but instead she sat down quietly and stared at the ground, her body trembling.

"I don't like *Onkel* Silas," Sheba whispered.

"Sheba, hush," hissed Norma, glancing nervously up at the woman sitting beside them to see if she'd heard.

But she hadn't heard, and a ripple of shock ran through Norma's chest. It was Prissy Raber. And although she was trying to hide it with a handkerchief held to her eyes, she was crying.

Chapter Four

Norma breathed a sigh of relief as she carried a stack of plates out to one of the tables on the Kings' big lawn. The shady oak trees surrounding the lawn made it the perfect spot to hold the post-church meal after the sermon on this sunny day, and Norma was grateful that the women and older girls always spent this time preparing for the first seating of the meal. At least that meant she had no choice but to leave Silas with her brothers and father for once.

Settling the plates on the table, she glanced across at another table nearby, and a pang of sorrow ran through her. It was groaning with desserts of all kinds – pies and cakes, cookies and tarts, their cheerful colors and sugary smell brightening the whole day. But for the first time almost since Norma could remember, not a single one of those dishes was her own.

Cutlery clattered on Norma's left. She looked up to see Prissy piling a bundle of knives and forks haphazardly on the table, her nose and eyes so red and pathetic that Norma could almost forgive her for courting Trevor. She gave a little sob, and Norma reached over, touching her arm.

"Prissy?" she said with genuine alarm. "What's the matter?"

Prissy mopped her eyes on her apron. "*Nee*, nothing," she said, forcing a smile.

"It doesn't look like nothing," said Norma gently.

Prissy's lower lip trembled, and Norma felt real concern. "You look so sad," she said. "What's wrong?"

"It's... it's my *mammi*," Prissy whispered.

Norma swallowed hard. The pain behind those words was all too familiar. "What about her?" she asked.

"She's not well. I want to help her," Prissy gulped. She mopped at her eyes. "It's been so hard being away from her. Everything has been hard since *Daed* died. She's all the way back in Pennsylvania, and I miss her so much, and now I've just gotten the news from my younger *shvestah* that she's gotten even sicker."

"Prissy... I had no idea." Norma felt a pang of guilt. She wrapped her arms around the slender girl, gathering her comfortingly into her ample embrace. She'd judged this girl so many times, yet she had no idea that Prissy was out here without any family to call her own. "I'm so sorry."

"*Danke*, Norma." Prissy drew back, wiping away another tear. "It's been a terrible day. So many things have happened..."

Her voice trailed off, and Norma tried to hide her suspicion. It sounded as though something else was bothering Prissy, too. Could it have something to do with Trevor? She pushed the thought away as quickly as she could, gripping Prissy's hand. "I'll be praying for you and your *mudder*."

"*Danke*," Prissy whispered. She sighed. "Pray for me and..." Stopping, she shook her head. "Just *danke*, Norma."

Norma watched her go, more suspicious than ever. What had happened between Prissy and Trevor?

As the men sat at the tables for the meal, Norma couldn't stop staring at Trevor. It was definitely better than staring at Silas – partitioned between Norma's father and brothers so that he couldn't cause too much havoc. Her mind spun, thoughts flying through it as she stared at the young man's sturdy back. He was quieter than usual; normally, he would laugh and joke with his friends. But today, he just gazed down at his bowl of apple cobbler, eating almost mechanically, as if his mind were a long way away. Once, he looked across the room to where Prissy sat, and Norma saw his shoulders slump.

He turned, and their eyes met. Norma felt a blush rising up from her very soul. She looked away quickly, her heart speeding up at the tiny contact of their gazes. It thumped so hard that she thought he might just hear it. Maybe he did, for a few minutes later, when the crowd of men rose and excused themselves from the tables, he made his way toward her as she headed for the her spot with the rest of the women and girls. For a moment, she wanted to flee. To hide, perhaps, but she couldn't possibly have concealed herself behind any of the other ladies, so she just pretended not to see him even though every cell of her was acutely aware that he was walking toward her.

"*Gut* afternoon, Norma," he said warmly. His voice was warm honey on hot toast.

Norma looked up at him, cool and composed. "It's nice to see you, Trevor," she said calmly. At least, that was what she had planned. What actually happened was that she swallowed too fast, almost choked on her own words, spluttered for a second and squeaked, "Hello!" in a raspy voice.

To his credit, Trevor didn't miss a beat. "I just thought I'd thank you for that delicious apple cobbler," he said. "I knew it must have been yours – it was absolutely *wunderlich*. *Danke* for always bringing such *gut* things to church."

Norma felt her flaming face blaze even redder. "I – I didn't bring the abble coppler," she said.

"The *what?*" said Trevor.

"Apple cobbler," Norma corrected herself with embarrassment. "I didn't bring it."

"You didn't? *Ach*, well – it was just so *gut*," said Trevor. "What about the chocolate chip cookies? I ate three of them."

"*Nee*." Norma hung her head, flooded with shame. "I didn't bring... well, anything." She bit her lip, wishing more than ever that she could just disappear.

"Oh." There was plain disappointment in Trevor's face. It clashed with her embarrassment and hung in the air between them like a fat cloud. Norma sneaked a glance up at Trevor's face, searching his eyes for signs that things were really over between him and Prissy. But she knew she could never ask.

"I'd better..." she began.

He spoke at the same time. "Well, I should..."

They paused, and the silence blossomed between them again.

"See you next week, Norma," Trevor said at last.

"See you," Norma squeaked back.

She turned to watch him disappear into the crowd of men in dark suits, aware that her heart had just turned a somersault. Because what she saw in Trevor's eyes was something she hadn't been expecting.

It was fascination.

Chapter Five

Sheba's laughter floated in through the open kitchen window, punctuating the slosh of dish water in the sink as Norma scrubbed at a greasy plate. She couldn't help smiling to herself, glancing up out of the window. It was a perfect Saturday afternoon, quiet and sunny; the steady thump of their old buggy horse's hooves on the soft grass of the field just by the house was a rhythmic punctuation to the quiet day. Ruben was walking the old horse, laughing as the animal moved in circles this way and that.

Norma remembered a time when she had also been entertained with her fat pony through that field, walking across the grass for no reason other than to enjoy the feeling of the sun on her face and the earth beneath her feet. Now, though, those days were long gone – gone with *Mamm* when she'd breathed her last. Norma leaned forward and tapped on the window with a knuckle. "Ruben!" she shouted. "Don't tire poor old Snowy out like that. He still has to take us to church tomorrow."

"Just a few more minutes, Norma," Sheba shouted back.

"Five minutes," Norma urged. She shook her head, turning back to the dishes. If her hands hadn't been soapy and wet, she would have rubbed her aching temples. She wondered if *Mamm* had ever felt like this: as if her whole life was nothing but a staggering, exhausted moving from one chore to the next. Her thoughts were interrupted by—

"NORMA!" roared Silas.

Norma jumped, almost dropping the glass she was washing. She wished Silas could just call out gently instead of bellowing like an angry bull.

"Coming, onkel!" she called. Wiping her hands on a dishcloth, she hurried to his room. *Please, not another bowel accident*, she thought to herself. Pulling open the door, she was relieved to see Silas sitting up in a dry bed, glaring at her over his book.

"What can I do for you?" she asked as politely as she could manage.

"I need a glass of water," said Silas.

"Certainly. I'll be right..."

There was a shriek from outside, and it froze Norma's blood. It wasn't the usual happy scream of a thirteen-year-old girl enjoying her play. There was pain in it, and it stabbed straight through Norma's heart. Not bothering to close the door behind her, she headed out of the house at a dead run, making for the field. What she saw made her heart scramble and thrum in all the wrong places. The horse was cantering off across the field, his reins hanging loose around his neck. And Ruben was running towards a small heap of dark blue dress lying on the grass.

"Sheba!" Norma yelled, redoubling her pace as best as she could.

"It's all right. It's all right, Sheba." Ruben's voice was shaking as he fell to his knees beside her.

Sheba was crying. At least, she was breathing, but Norma's heart still felt wild. The little girl was lying curled up on her side, her skirts inelegantly sprawled on the grass, both hands clasped around her left ankle. Tears were streaming down her cheeks, but her face was ashen.

"What happened?" Norma gasped.

"A bee stung him," said Ruben, indicating the horse. "He reared and knocked into Sheba – she fell." He clutched his sister's arms. "Sheba, what hurts?"

"My ankle," Sheba whispered. "My ankle."

Norma gripped her fingers, trying to work them loose from her ankle. "Let go, *shvestah*," she said. "I need to see what's wrong."

Sheba let go, and Norma felt her heart flip. The ankle joint looked loose, disconnected, a bone jutting against the skin in a way that she was certain it shouldn't.

"Norma?" Sheba whimpered.

"It's all right, *liebchen*," said Norma. She laid a hand on Sheba's shoulder, working to her keep fears under control. "We'll just have to take you to the hospital."

"I'll get *Daed*." Ruben lurched to his feet and ran off toward the house.

"You'll be all right, Sheba," said Norma. "Don't worry. You'll be all right."

She prayed her words were true. And she had never missed *Mamm* more than in that moment.

There were forty-six big blue tiles on the floor of the hospital corridor. Forty-nine, if you counted the partial ones in three of the corners. At least, that was guessing that there was just one tile under Norma's chair. She didn't want to look silly by leaning over to check.

She counted them again, just to be sure, although she'd counted them a hundred times since Sheba had been taken into the hospital room and the doctor had gone sweeping inside, with his mustache and lab coat and golden watch. Now, Norma sat outside, waiting. Ruben, Thaddeus, and Abel had stayed at home to watch over the farm. She could just see *Daed*'s familiar, sturdy figure through the frosted glass.

She had started to count the tiles again when the door opened. Sitting up, Norma watched the doctor march back out again, his expression unreadable. *Daed* followed, looking old and tired.

"What does he say?" Norma asked.

Daed sagged down into a chair beside her.

"It could have been worse," he said. "Sheba's broken her ankle, but it's a clean break. The doctor says it'll heal without needing a surgery."

Norma felt herself relax, if only a little. "That's *gut* news then, *Daed*."

"*Jah*, it is. She had me worried." *Daed* put an arm around Norma's shoulders. "I think she had you worried there, too."

"That she did," said Norma. "Does she need a cast?"

"*Jah*, I'm afraid so. She'll wear a cast and need to use crutches to get around for six weeks or so," said *Daed*.

Six weeks. The words made Norma feel suddenly exhausted. She leaned her head back against the wall, the adrenaline seeping out of her. "She was my only help around the *haus*," she whispered.

"Norma." *Daed*'s tone was chiding. "Your *shvestah* is in pain. You should be grateful that she isn't more badly hurt."

Tears stung Norma's eyes. She turned her face away, hoping her father wouldn't see them, but she couldn't hide her shaking shoulders. *Daed*'s arm tightened around them.

"Norma?" he said, more gently. "What's wrong?"

"I'm sorry," she whispered. "Of course, I'm glad Sheba is all right. But with Silas and the *haus* and..." She stopped, looking down into her lap, feeling shame rise in her heart. "I know I should be able to cope with everything. But sometimes, I just can't."

Daed sighed. "*Ach*, I know that Silas can be difficult, *dochtah*. And *danke* for the way that you care for him." He squeezed her shoulders tightly. "I know you miss your *mudder*."

Norma looked up at him, surprised. He never talked about *Mamm*. *Daed* tried to smile. "It's only for six weeks, though. Once the pain is under control, maybe Sheba will be able to start helping you again."

"*Danke*," said Norma, surprised by his understanding. She snuggled a little closer under his arm. "I love you."

He kissed her *kapp*. "I love you, too. And I'll help in the *haus* where I can."

Norma knew that he meant it, but she also knew there was no getting around the fact that the next six weeks were not going to be easy. Still, maybe things would be all right.

Maybe Silas would go home soon.

Chapter Six

When Norma walked into the kitchen with a tray of dirty dishes from Silas's room, the smell of burning toast was almost as pervasive as the smoke hanging in the air.

"*Daed!*" she yelped, running to the oven and turning off the gas. She pulled the door open, and a cloud of black smoke rose into the air from the charred bits of bread lying on the grill.

"*Ach, nee.*" *Daed* ran in, holding a mop. It looked utterly out of place in his hand, and as he stared at the oven, Norma realized she'd never seen her father looking insecure before. "I'm sorry!"

"What were you doing?" Norma asked, grabbing an oven glove and fishing out the grill. The bread, or what was left of it, was reduced to something resembling charcoal.

"Making... toast," said *Daed*, uncertainly.

Norma stared at the toast. Then she stared at the mop, which was sodden and dripping with what was very clearly dish-washing liquid. She stared up at *Daed*, and his utterly forlorn expression was just far too much for her. She burst out laughing.

"What?" *Daed* demanded, immediately indignant.

"*Ach, Daed*, you tried," said Norma. She tossed the burned bread into the garbage. "Come on – let's make some toast in the pan. Maybe you could fry some eggs?"

Daed squared his shoulders like Norma had just given him some vital mission. "I'll do that," he said with determination. "Oh, and how do I get the suds off the washroom floor?"

Norma stifled a giggle. "Don't worry, *Daed*. I'll take care of it later."

She kept a careful eye on her father as he started cracking eggs into a pan. Even though his help around the house had caused more chaos than anything else in the past few days, Norma couldn't express to him how much she appreciated it. By the time the boys had come in from the fields and helped Sheba to hobble down the stairs on her crutches, *Daed* had broken two of the yolks, dropped a plate, and nearly set fire to the curtains, but everyone was laughing as they sat down to breakfast.

At least this was the one time when Norma could sit with her family: Silas demanded his bowl of oatmeal at seven sharp, while the rest of her family was still outside caring for the animals.

The breakfast dishes had been piled into the sink and Norma's father and brothers were back outside again within a few minutes, getting in a second cutting of hay.

"Come on, Sheba," said Norma, taking her sister's arm. "Let me help you back up the stairs."

"*Danke*, Norma." Sheba's smile was starting to return to its usual level of sass. "Soon I'll be able to manage them on my own again."

"Of course, you will. And then you can start to do your chores again, too," said Norma, laughing.

Sheba pouted. "Maybe not that soon, then," she said, with a cheeky grin.

Norma just shook her head, helping her little sister up the flight of stairs and back to bed. The little girl's face was still pale with pain, and Norma made sure she had her medication and some books to read while she sat with her cast-bound ankle raised on a pillow. She was just fluffing up Sheba's pillows to make her comfortable when their dog barked downstairs, and there was a knock at the door.

"Coming!" Norma shouted. "Are you all right, Sheba?"

"I'm fine," said Sheba, waving a hand. "Go and see who it is. Maybe it's Patty, then she can come and visit me."

Hurrying down the stairs, Norma hoped that it was Sheba's friend, and not just for Sheba's sake. She still had all of those dishes to do and a basketful of laundry to get onto the line before getting lunch ready, and no doubt Silas would soon be yelling for attention. Norma didn't have time to entertain guests. A little breathless, she reached the front door and pulled it open, and the whole world stopped.

The wild spin that her life had been ever since Silas arrived came to an abrupt halt. Suddenly, Norma was taking in every detail. The scent of the lilies growing in the pot on the porch. The stirring of the summer breeze, causing the trees to hum in a throaty rustle. The way the sunlight caught the dark curls that peeked out from under Trevor Schwartz's hat, making them look back-lit with gold. The depth of his green eyes as he started to smile, a tiny dimple appearing in each cheek. The left one was a little deeper than the right, and one of his teeth was ever so slightly crooked. It was a minute imperfection, but it still made Norma's heart turn over.

"Uh... *gut* morning," said Trevor, his smile widening.

The world suddenly returned to its normal speed, leaving Norma breathless and a little off balance. She grabbed at the door frame.

"Trevor," she said. "What are you doing here?" The words came out harsh. She blinked, shaking her head. "I mean, what a lovely surprise! I mean, I didn't expect you to be here. Why are you here? Why aren't you there?" She wasn't making sense even to herself. "What?" she demanded, more of herself than anyone else.

Trevor stared at her in silence. That cloud of discomfort was growing between them again.

Norma drew herself up as well as she could. "Can I start again?"

To her surprise, Trevor laughed out loud. "*Jah*, please do."

Norma cleared her throat. "*Gut* morning, Trevor," she said. "It's nice to see you."

"It's nice to see you, too," he replied. He held up something loaf-shaped and smelling sweetly fruity, wrapped in a dishcloth. "*Mamm* heard about your *shvestah* hurting her ankle, and she sent me over with this banana bread. She thought she might appreciate it."

"Sheba loves banana bread," said Norma.

Trevor nodded. "I remember you telling me so when you brought some to church a few months ago," he said. "It was delicious, but *Mamm*'s recipe is pretty *gut*, too."

"You remember?" Norma asked in wonder. It seemed so improbable, but she remembered it too, especially his smile as he'd lifted a slice to his nose and breathed its scent.

"Of course, I do," said Trevor. "Is this a bad time, or may I come in?"

"*Jah, jah*! Come on in." Norma yanked the door open a little too violently. It clonked her solidly on the forehead, and she staggered back, trying to pretend that it didn't hurt.

"Ouch!" said Trevor. "Are you all right?"

"*Jah*, I'm fine," she said, her eyes watering. She sniffed the tears back. "Come on in – do you want some coffee? Or tea? Or cocoa? Not cocoa. It's not cold out. Lemonade?"

Trevor laughed. "Lemonade sounds *wunderlich*. It's not a long walk, but the sun is warm today."

"It *is* warm," agreed Norma, leading him into the kitchen. She took the banana bread. "Well, it isn't winter, I guess."

"So you said," said Trevor, but the look on his face was gentle, almost amused. It made Norma feel a little better, even though she knew she was blundering. She managed to grab a glass from the cupboard without mishap and took some homemade lemonade from the refrigerator.

"So how is Sheba?" he asked as Norma poured the lemonade.

"*Ach*, she's *gut*. Well, her ankle is broken, so not that *gut*," said Norma. "But she's in less pain than she was. The doctor says that it should heal well without any trouble."

"*Ach*, that's *wunderlich*," said Trevor. "I remember it was very painful when I fell out of a tree and broke my arm when I was little. Tell Sheba that it'll get better — and banana bread helps."

"I'm sure it does." Norma laughed, loving how much easier it was becoming to talk to Trevor. She picked up a shirt that was lying on the table. "I'm sorry — I would love to sit and visit with you, but do you mind if I patch this while you drink your lemonade?"

"Not at all," said Trevor. "I can understand that you must be busy."

Norma sat down and picked up a needle and thread. "Ruben is terrible when it comes to his clothes — always getting caught up on something and tearing them. *Mamm* used to say he'd grow out of it, but he was a little boy then, and he's nearly a man now."

"You sound like my *Mamm*. I always need patches or darning."

"*Ach*, I would love to..." Norma just managed to bite off the end of what was almost a disastrously embarrassing and forward sentence. ... *patch your clothes for you one day*. She felt her face heating up as she tried to save the sentence. "Uh... I'd love to know how your *Mamm* does it all. I only have five people to care for, and you have, what, eight siblings?"

"*Jah*, that's right." Trevor smiled. "But three of them are *shvestahs*, and they help *Mamm* around the house a lot. I don't know how you get around to caring for your whole family like you do."

"It's hard now that Sheba is hurt," Norma admitted, gazing at him. It was the first time anyone outside her family had noticed her efforts.

"Your *onkel* seems like he can be..." Trevor searched for words.

"A lot of work?" Norma suggested.

"I was going to say, 'a bit grumpy'," said Trevor.

Norma laughed. "*Onkel* Silas is a *gut* man, I'm sure," she said. "He just needs some help in his old age – like all of us will eventually, I suppose."

"NORMA!"

The roar from the sewing room made Trevor jump so hard that his chair squeaked on the floor. Norma sighed, lowering the shirt. "Speaking of him," she said. "Sounds like he wants something.'

"You're halfway through a stitch there," Trevor pointed out. He got to his feet. "Let me go and see what he needs."

"Are you sure?" said Norma, glancing at him in surprise.

"*Jah,* of course. I'll just see what he wants," said Trevor.

"*Ach, danke,* Trevor. I appreciate the help."

Trevor left the room, and Norma permitted herself a lovesick little smile as she went on sewing the patch on Ruben's shirt. She had been watching Trevor for years, but she could feel her crush on him growing into something deeper with every word they exchanged. And if he'd come here alone, maybe that was a sign that he and Prissy really had broken up.

Finishing the patch, Norma put the shirt down and frowned. Trevor still hadn't come back yet. Her stomach flipped over as she wondered if Silas had had another accident. Maybe Trevor had simply run away in terror – or, worse, maybe he was helping the nasty old man. She jumped to her feet and hurried toward the sewing room, opening her mouth to call his name, but what she heard stopped her.

"... Norma," Silas was saying. "Why, I can hardly believe I haven't died from this filthy, disease-riddled room."

Norma slowed. She tiptoed closer, seeing that the door was open a crack. Peering through the crack, she could see that Silas was sitting up in bed, his face scarlet as he launched into a full tirade.

"All day, I sit alone here in this room, you know," he was saying. "Starving and thirsty – I can barely ask for a cup of water in this place. My *brudder* came and took me out of my home where I was happy and dragged me out here to cage me. Why, I don't know. Things have gone downhill so badly around here since his wife died. That girl of his barely lifts a finger to create some kind of order in this *haus*."

Chapter Seven

Norma stifled a gasp. Silas was talking to Trevor, and the young man was listening attentively. His back was to Norma, but she knew that if she could see his face, it would be filled with disgust.

"Is that so?" Trevor said.

"I'm telling you so," said Silas. "Get away from here as quickly as you can. That *maidel* is the laziest person I've ever seen in my life – look at the state of this *haus*! Look at the state of me. It's no wonder the younger girl hurt herself with the neglect she suffers."

That was the last straw. Norma strode forward and reached for the door, ready to give Silas a piece of her mind, when there was a piercing shriek from upstairs. *Sheba*. Norma felt her heart squeeze. She'd have to fight with Silas later.

"Sheba?" she called, running up the stairs as fast as she could. "Sheba, *liebchen*, are you all right?"

"In here," a small voice sobbed from the bathroom.

Norma pulled open the upstairs bathroom door. Sheba was lying on the floor in an ignominious heap. Her crutches had skidded away across the tiles from her, and her dress was soaked. "I was just trying to wash my hands," she whimpered. "I slipped on the water."

"*Ach*, Sheba! You should have called me to help you," said Norma, grabbing the crutches. She handed them to her sister and helped her back onto her feet. "Are you all right?"

"*Jah*, I think so," said Sheba shakily, rubbing her bumped elbow. "C-can you just walk back to my room with me, please?"

"Of course," said Norma tenderly. "Come on. Let's get you back to bed."

It seemed to take an age to get Sheba back to her room, and with every painful step, Norma was acutely aware that Silas was just downstairs telling Trevor what a terrible human being she was. She got Sheba tucked back into her room and changed into a dry dress, then hurried downstairs, her feet pounding on the passage.

"Trevor?" she called out, breathlessly. "Trevor?"

She yanked open the sewing room door. Silas was sitting in

bed, reading. He gave her a furious look. "What do you want?"

"Where is he?" Norma gasped.

"Gone," said Silas. "Just as horrified by the state of this *haus* as I am." He snorted. "Except that he can get away from it."

Norma stared at him. A wave of anger rose in her chest, threatening to overwhelm her, but she took a deep breath. *It's only for a few weeks,* she told herself. *Just a few weeks.* She couldn't think of anything remotely kind to say to Silas, so she didn't say anything. She just stepped quietly out of the room and closed the door behind her. And then she covered her face and allowed herself to cry, wholeheartedly, and as silently as she could.

Whatever chance she'd possibly had with Trevor was gone now. Silas had ruined it. Just like he was busy ruining everything else in her life.

Norma forced her hands to be gentle as she tugged Silas's socks over his nasty yellow feet. She gently folded them over at the top the way he liked them. The left one was a little askew, so she gave it a tug to straighten it out.

"Ouch!" Silas roared, yanking up his leg so that his foot narrowly missed Norma's face. "What are you doing to me, woman?"

"Sorry, *Onkel*," said Norma through gritted teeth. She seized his foot, pulled it back down, and smoothed out the sock. "I didn't want it to be uncomfortable for you."

"Then perhaps you should have washed my socks better," snapped Silas. "They're stiff with dirt."

Norma knew the words were nonsense, but they still stung. She grabbed for Silas's shoes and stuffed his feet into them, lacing them up. "Is that tight enough for you?" she growled.

"*Nee*, of course not. They're much too tight. I can't feel my toes," Silas whined. "Why don't you just kill me and get it over with, you hateful *maidel*?"

Norma swallowed back her anger. It slid down her throat, bitter and stinging, like bile. She loosened the shoes and straightened up.

"I'll be right back with your tea," she said primly, and strode back out of the room before Silas could say anything more.

Her family was just sitting down to breakfast when she walked into the kitchen. Their merry chatter normally lifted her spirits, but today it felt like it was just bouncing right off her, incapable of penetrating the black cloud that surrounded her heart. She turned off the heat under the pot of oatmeal on the stove and gave it a last stir. "Breakfast's ready."

"I took bowls out already," said *Daed*, touching her arm. "Why don't you sit down for a minute? I'll bring in the food."

Norma wanted to hug him, but she knew she would start crying if she did. *"Danke, Daed,"* she said, smiling tearfully.

She took her place beside Abel, who noticed her unhappy expression and gave her a friendly little bump with his elbow.

"What's wrong?" he whispered as their siblings went to get their oatmeal. Norma shook her head mutely, not ready to talk about it in case she said terrible things about Silas – which she knew she shouldn't.

The family sat down, and *Daed* lowered his head, closing his eyes. Taking their cue from him, the rest of the group followed suit. Their traditional silent moment of grace wound its way through Norma's mind, almost automatic. She tried to make her heart pray with sincerity, but it was so deeply entrenched in what was going on with Silas and Trevor that praying seemed harder than usual.

"There we go," said *Daed*, grace over. *"Danke* for breakfast, Norma."

"Danke," murmured the rest of the family.

Norma spooned some oatmeal into her mouth, barely tasting it. It seemed to turn into sand on her tongue when *Daed* cleared his throat. "There's something that we have to discuss," he said.

Norma's head snapped up. Nothing good ever started like that. "What's wrong?"

Daed reached over and laid his hand over hers. "It's Silas," he said.

"What about him?" Norma tried to keep the venom out of her tone, but she could feel a surge of rage in her heart.

"*Kinner*, when we first went to fetch Silas, it was believing that he'd just had a bout of illness and needed a few weeks' care to recuperate. We thought we could take him back home once he was feeling better," said *Daed*. His eyes dwelt on Norma. "But I was getting concerned that he didn't seem to be getting any better."

Norma swallowed hard.

"*Nee*," she said reluctantly. "He's not getting better. If anything, he's getting worse... more frail. He used to be able to tie his own shoelaces, but now he can barely pull up his trousers. I have to help him with everything." She heard bitterness leak into her tone and took a steadying breath. "He's definitely not getting better."

"I think Silas is frailer – and much sicker – than we realized," said *Daed* quietly. "In fact, when I took him to town last week, I wasn't just letting him get some fresh air." He took a deep breath. "I took him to the hospital for tests. And it's not *gut* news."

Norma's heart flipped. Just when things couldn't get any worse...

"What's wrong with him?" asked Abel softly.

"It's cancer," said *Daed*. "There's nothing they can do. They suggested putting him in a nursing home, but we don't abandon our family. Neither do we have that kind of money." He swallowed. "Silas isn't going to go home. He's going to stay here with us for the rest of his life – and we're not sure how long that's going to be."

Norma closed her eyes, feeling a rush of selfish anger. She tried to push it away as well as she could. *What's wrong with you?* she chided herself. *Your onkel is dying and all you can think about is yourself.*

Daed seemed to read her mind. "I know this is going to be hard on all of us, but Silas has nowhere else to go," he said gently. "We can't abandon him in his old age."

Norma opened her eyes. "Of course not," she said quickly. "We'll care for him, *Daed*. It's all right."

"*Danke,* Norma," said *Daed*, squeezing her hand.

"But what about his farm?" asked Thaddeus. "He doesn't have any sons to give it to. Or even a wife. His neighbors won't want to care for it forever."

"That's what I also need to talk to you about." *Daed* took a deep breath. "Most of Silas's belongings are still on the farm, and while most of his animals have been sold, his farm still needs to be put on the market as well. I planned for Ruben, Thaddeus, and I to go over to the farm and put it up for sale and fetch the things he still needs. Abel, you'll stay here with

Norma and Sheba." He gave Norma an apologetic look before gazing at Abel and Sheba. "I want both of you to try your best to help Norma around the *haus* and be considerate towards her. She has a lot to do, especially with Silas to care for."

"*Jah, Daed,*" murmured both Abel and Sheba, although Sheba gave her crutches a nervous glance.

"*Gut,*" said *Daed.* "We'll leave on Wednesday morning." He squeezed Norma's hand. "Hopefully, we'll be back soon, *liebchen,*" he added softly.

Norma nodded, and her eyes filled with tears. The hope that she'd had – of Silas going home in a few weeks – was shattered. Her dreams with Trevor were gone. And to make matters worse, *Daed* was going to leave.

Just when things couldn't get any worse, they did.

Chapter Eight

It was a good thing that Snowy knew his own way to town by now, because Norma didn't have the energy to hold the reins tightly. They hung loosely on the old horse's back as he mustered a slow trot, his hooves beating a steady, lulling rhythm on the tarmac. It was enough to make Norma want to fall asleep where she sat on the front seat of the buggy. She leaned back, feeling the warm sun on her face and arms, the gentle breeze stirred by Snowy's movement. *Daed* had been apologetic when he'd reminded Norma to take Sheba to the doctor for a check-up on her ankle, but truth be told, the few hours away from home were a welcome reprieve from Silas's constant grumbling.

If Norma had hoped that knowing his time was limited would make the old man change his ways, those hopes had been quickly dashed. Silas was as determined as ever to make her life a misery. She wondered if he was in pain, if that was what made him angry. She vowed silently not to become snappish herself, even though it was hard at times.

"Norma?" Sheba said beside her. "Are you still awake?"

"*Jah, jah.*" Norma sat up, giving Sheba a reassuring smile. "Sorry. Silas woke me up a few times last night to go to the bathroom."

"How long do you think he'll take to die?"

"Sheba!" Norma remonstrated. "That's not a nice thing to ask."

"I'm sorry," said Sheba, shrugging her shoulders with teenage bluntness. "I still don't like him, even though he's old and sick."

Norma sighed. "You don't need to like him, Sheba," she said, turning Snowy in at the entrance to the doctor's parking lot. "But you do need to treat him with love and respect."

She tied Snowy to a hitching rail and gave him a nosebag to nibble on while she helped Sheba across the pavement and toward the doctor's office. Sheba was managing her crutches well now and shook off Norma's hand when they reached the steps into the waiting room.

"I'm all right," she said.

"You sure?" said Norma.

"I'm sure. It's much better." Leaning on one crutch, Sheba used the other to bump the door open and hobbled confidently inside.

Norma followed her, and once again, despite the exhaustion sucking at her spirit, her world jolted to a halt. He was there, sitting in one of the uncomfortable chairs that lined the wall of the waiting room, his legs crossed, fingers interlocked on his right knee. *Trevor.* He looked up when they came in, and his eyes widened when he saw Norma. She froze, not knowing which way to look, feeling her face turn scarlet. What was he thinking as he stared at her? She tore her eyes away from him and aimed them down at her apron instead, and she saw that there was a small coffee stain on her skirt. She scolded herself inwardly.

"Trevor," said Sheba. "It's nice to see you here." She hobbled over to the chair beside him and plopped down. "At least there's another Amish face around."

"Hello, Sheba," said Trevor. Norma knew his eyes were following her as she took her place beside her sister. "Hello, Norma," he said softly.

"*Gut* morning," Norma whispered. "Are you sick?" She swallowed. "I mean, what are you doing here? I mean..." She groaned inwardly. "How are you?"

"I'm fine."

"But you're at the doctor's," said Norma.

"*Jah*, but I'm not sick," said Trevor. "Or hurt. Or anything." His cheeks turned pink, and Norma felt awful. Why was he so awkward around her? Did he pity her? Was he dismayed by her?

The office door opened, and a woman that Norma recognized as Trevor's mother came out. Her nose and eyes were red, and she gave a quiet, damp cough. Trevor jumped to his feet. "What did he say, *Mamm*?" he asked, his voice heavy with concern and compassion.

"Oh, it's just the flu, *liebchen*," said Trevor's mother. "I have to stay in bed for a few days and take some medicine, but I'll be fine." Her eyes traveled to Norma, and she gave a small smile. "I'm just going to walk across the street to the drugstore. You can wait here for me."

"I'll go with you," Trevor said.

"*Nee*, I'll be fine." His mother gave a hoarse laugh. "You stay here and visit our neighbors."

"Sheba Glick," called the receptionist as soon as Trevor's mother left.

"Here!" Sheba scrambled to her feet.

"I'm coming," said Norma, grabbing Sheba's arm.

She shook her hand away. "It's all right, Norma. I'll go in myself. I'm not a little child, you know."

With that, Trevor and Norma were left alone in the waiting

room, although it felt like the cloud between them had grown to the size of an elephant. Norma shifted tremulously, not knowing where to look. She stared at the floor with her hands resting in her lap.

Trevor spoke after a silence that seemed to last an eon. "I... I'm sorry I left in such a hurry the other day."

Tears burned Norma's throat. She swallowed them down. "I don't blame you," she whispered.

"What do you mean?" asked Trevor.

Norma looked up at him. "Why would you want to stay? After the things my *onkel* said to you."

Trevor's brows were knotted in consternation. "Silas asked me to take your *dat* a message out in the fields," he said slowly. "By the time I'd found him in the bottom hay field, I was late for lunch. I had to get home quickly."

"Oh," said Norma. Her world tilted slightly. "That's why you left?"

"Why else would I leave so rudely?" said Trevor, clearly puzzled.

Norma's heart gave a brisk double-thump of hope in her chest, but she crushed it down. *You're going to care for Silas for the rest of your life*, she told herself with exasperation born from experience. *There's no room for Trevor.* Besides, he hadn't said anything yet about what Silas had told him about her.

"I-I'm sorry your *mamm* is ill," she said.

"She doesn't feel at all well, but I'm sure she'll be recover," said Trevor. "And Sheba?"

"Getting much better now." Norma tried to smile, but she thought she saw judgment in Trevor's eyes as he looked at her.

"*Ach*, that's *gut* to hear," said Trevor.

"Trevor?" his mother's hoarse voice called from the hallway. "I'm ready."

"Well, I guess I'd better go," said Trevor. He got up, wiping his hands on his pants. "Oh, I heard that your *dat* and two of your *brudders* will be away for a while. Let me know if there's anything I can do to help you."

"*Danke*," said Norma. "Have a *gut* day."

Her heart was still pounding as Trevor walked away, but she forced herself not to watch him go.

Just as she forced herself to believe that his friendly offer was nothing but neighborliness.

Norma had seldom been so happy to see the white shape of Dinah's *kapp* heading up the driveway toward her. She sat back, her hands still buried in the laundry tub, and watched as her friend made her way up the lawn. It was a breezy day, and Dinah kept one hand on her *kapp* to keep it under control.

"*Gut* morning!" Dinah chirped, still halfway across the drive.

Norma smiled. Being engaged suited Dinah; her cheeks were bright pink, her eyes alive. "You look so happy," she said as Dinah reached her.

"I wish I could say the same for you," said Dinah. "Things are busy with the wedding preparations, but when I saw you in town with Sheba yesterday, I knew I needed to stop in and check on you." She held up the basket on her arm. "I brought a casserole for your dinner, but it looks like you're going to be busy with this for a while." Putting the basket on the lawn, Dinah rolled up her sleeves. "Let me give you a hand."

"*Ach*, Dinah, *danke*," said Norma. "That will be *wunderlich*. The wringer washer ain't working properly so I've been forced to do the washing the old-fashioned way."

Dinah knelt down beside Norma and held out a hand. Norma handed her a soapy pair of Abel's trousers, and her friend buried it in the rinse tub. "How are things with your *dat* and *brudders* out of town?"

"Awful," Norma admitted. "Sheba's trying to help around the *haus*, but she's in school all day. And Abel is busy doing all the work on the farm. At least I have less laundry to do with only four people in the *haus* instead of seven, but Silas is getting more frail – and more demanding than ever." She smiled. "But let's not complain. Tell me about the wedding."

"*Ach*, I'm so excited." Dinah gave a happy little squeal. "It's only six weeks to go. Every time I see a sign of autumn coming, I get more excited. I'm so fond of Joel, Norma. It's going to be such a blessing to be wed." She paused. "Speaking of such things, I know you and Trevor didn't have a *gut* meeting the other day, but I thought I'd tell you that you were right in what you'd guessed. Prissy has gone back to Pennsylvania to care for her *mudder*, and she and Trevor aren't courting anymore."

"I feel sorry for Prissy," said Norma. "I had no idea about her *mudder*."

"*Jah*, but maybe this could be your chance with Trevor."

"Maybe. I don't know. I saw him in town yesterday, and he told me he left in a hurry because Silas asked him to give a message to my *dat*," said Norma. "Still, Silas said awful things about me. I don't think Trevor sees me the same as he used to."

"You don't know that," said Dinah.

"I guess I don't." Norma sighed. "His *mudder* has the flu, Dinah."

Dinah gave her a sympathetic look. "She'll be all right. I know you're worried about it, considering what happened to your *mudder*, but don't be afraid, Norma. It's just the usual bug that goes around at this time of year – both of my little *brudders* have it as well. Hopefully Joel doesn't get it – he's like a grumpy old bear when he's sick." She laughed. "Oh, and maybe Sheba will be around the *haus* to help you more often, too."

"How so?" asked Norma.

"The teacher is sick," said Dinah. "My *brudders* told me. She's not going to teach tomorrow." She smiled. "Unless you take her spot."

Norma lowered the shirt she was washing. "What on earth do you mean?"

"You taught for a few weeks four or five years ago," said Dinah. "And the *kinner* loved you."

"And I loved teaching," said Norma. "But I can't get away from here, Dinah. Not with Sheba, and the *haus*, and Silas..." She felt her eyes filled with tears and turned her face away. "I can't do it," she whispered.

"Maybe you need to," said Dinah gently. "You need to have a rest from all this, Norma. You're going to fall apart, and what then? Your family needs you."

"That's exactly why I can't teach," said Norma. "They need me."

"They'll need you for many years to come," Dinah reminded her. "You need to take some care of yourself to be in this for the long haul. I think you should talk to the deacons and do it."

"Maybe," Norma murmured, turning back to the laundry. Dinah was right – she wasn't sure how much longer she could keep this up.

Chapter Nine

"My heart rejoices, rejoices in Thee, O Lord," Norma sang quietly under her breath as she strode up the driveway. "How magnificent Your works. How truly great You are." She gave a little skip up the porch steps and twirled in place, giggling in excitement. *"Danke, Gott,* for what You have done today," she whispered.

She couldn't wait to tell Abel and Sheba all about her meeting with the deacons and how they told her she could act as a substitute teacher for the next two weeks. She couldn't wait to share with them what it would mean to her. Opening the front door, she strode inside. "Abel? Sheba? You won't believe what—"

Norma stopped. The house echoed with noise, but the sound

was anything but joyous. It was Sheba, and she was crying hard.

"Sheba?" Norma cried, hurrying towards the source of the sound, which seemed to be near the sewing room. "Sheba, what's wrong?"

Sheba stormed out of the sewing room, nearly knocking Norma over. Norma grabbed her shoulders. "Sheba?" she questioned.

"Leave me alone!" Sheba yelled. She wrenched her shoulders free and hobbled off as quickly as her crutches could carry her. Horrified, Norma stepped into the sewing room. The pungent smell of urine filled the room, and her brother Abel was standing in the middle of the floor. His expression was utterly helpless as he stared, aghast, at Silas. The old man was lying in bed, and everything was utterly soaked – the sheets, the covers, the quilt, his clothes.

Abel looked up as Norma came in. "Norma," he said, relieved. "Thank goodness, you're here."

Norma stared mutely for a few seconds. As high as her heart had been soaring just a few minutes ago, it now crashed to the earth and shattered in a cloud of shards. Tears welled in her eyes, and she let them flow, but she held back her sobs as she stepped in and quietly began to strip Silas and the bed of the wet clothing and bedding. She could hear him ranting at her, as if at a distance; the world just hurt far too much for him to be able to add to that pain.

The tears continued to drip down her cheeks as she threw all the dirty laundry into a basket, dressed Silas in clean clothes, made the bed and tucked him back in again as he railed at her. Only when he was clean and dry did she walk to the kitchen and allow herself to slump down in the nearest chair and lay her head on her arms on the table. She was so tired, she felt as though she was going to melt into a little pool on the floor.

"Norma?"

Abel had been watching her wordlessly. Norma felt a childish desire to be alone. She tucked her arms around her face even though it was much too late to hide her tears.

"Norma." Abel sat down beside her, resting a hand on the small of her back. "What's the matter?"

"I'm just tired," Norma whispered.

"This is more than just tired." Abel tugged at her arms, encouraging her to look up at him. "You look so discouraged. I'm sorry. I should have just done – well, what you did. I was just – sort of horrified for a minute there. And he said some horrible things to Sheba. I don't know how..." He paused. "I don't know how you care for him when he's so cruel to you."

"He's old and sick," Norma whispered, wiping her eyes. "Horrible and spiteful, too, but he needs me. There's nothing I can do about that."

"But that's not what's bothering you, is it?" asked Abel.

Norma shook her head.

"What is it?" Abel hugged her one-armed. "Come on, *shvestah*. You know you can tell me."

Norma gave him a watery smile. "The deacons said *jah*," she whispered. "They'll let me teach for two weeks."

"But that's *wunderlich*, Norma."

"*Nee*, it's not," said Norma. "I'd rather they'd said *nee*. Then I wouldn't have to go back and tell them I can't do it."

"But why not?" asked Abel.

Norma gave a harsh laugh. "Look at what happened when I was away for just a morning" she said. "Sheba was crying, Silas and his bedding were soaked, and you were lost. I can't do that to you three."

"*Jah*, you can," said Abel.

"Who will take care of Silas?" Norma demanded. "Sheba's on crutches. I don't know why I ever thought that I could take on teaching for two weeks." She sighed, trying to calm herself. "It was just a silly dream. Don't worry about it." She wiped her eyes dry and got to her feet. "I'll get started on lunch."

"Norma, wait." Abel grabbed her arm. "Teaching won't take that long, will it? Only the mornings and a bit of the afternoons. You could still do it." He gritted his teeth, steeling himself. "I'll take care of Silas."

"You?" Norma stared at him. "You hate Silas."

"Well, 'hate' is a bit of a strong word," said Abel. "But more to the point, you're my *shvestah*, and I love you." He squeezed Norma's arm.

Norma felt tears in her eyes again, but this time, they were tears of gratitude. "Abel, are you sure?"

"I'm perfectly sure, *shvestah*." Abel grinned. "Go and enjoy these two weeks of teaching. You'll find a way to pay it back to me."

"I will!" Norma threw her arms around his neck. "*Danke, brudder. Danke* so much."

Abel gently hugged her back.

It was surprising how well Sheba was getting around on her crutches. She crossed the schoolroom floor at the same time as her band of friends, hopping over to Norma's desk effortlessly.

"You coming, Norma?" she called. "Emma's *vadder* is here with the buggy to pick us up."

Norma looked up from the pile of papers on the desk. She gazed at Sheba, feeling another wave of exhaustion wash over her. "*Nee, danke,* Sheba," she said. "I've still got to finish my lesson plans for tomorrow. Will you make a start on dinner for me? I'll walk home – it's not far, and it's a nice day."

Sheba shrugged. "Sure." She paused. "Are you all right?"

Norma resisted the urge to rub her temples. Her siblings had made a big sacrifice to give her this time to teach, and she forced a smile. "*Jah*, of course. Just a little busy. See you later."

"All right. See you," said Sheba.

She headed out with her gaggle of friends, and Norma sighed, turning back to her papers. She didn't want to admit to Sheba and Abel that coming to the schoolhouse hadn't been the magic cure for her tiredness and frustration that she'd hoped for. The worries of home seemed to follow her like a shadow; instead of enjoying her time with the children, she found herself worrying over how Abel was managing with Silas.

Sighing, Norma finished with her lesson plans and left the schoolhouse, locking the door behind her. Maybe she should tell the deacons that she couldn't finish her last week of teaching. It would hurt her heart, but maybe it would be the right thing to do. She hoped that the walk home would straighten out her thoughts.

The landscape seemed to be trying to soothe her as she made her way down the lane. The hedges were still mostly green, but their edges were tinged with gold; a few leaves had fallen from the trees and scattered on the verges, their edges curling with fall's first quiet touch. Norma took a deep breath of the fragrant air. Soon it would be harvest time, and there would be plenty of work to do. There would be golden colors and weddings and apple pie. Her heart ached as she wondered when last she'd had a chance to bake something more interesting than bread.

"Why the long face?" a voice asked from her right.

Norma jumped, turning. Trevor was walking along beside her. She wondered how long he'd been there. "Oh – hello," she said, too surprised to feel embarrassed. "Sorry. I was deep in thought."

"I can see that." Trevor smiled, his manner easy. "My *brudder* told me to tell you that you're his favorite teacher, by the way."

Norma smiled. "That's nice to hear. Where are you off to?"

"Oh, nowhere in particular," said Trevor.

It seemed like the most natural thing in the world to fall into step with him, heading home through the fragrant afternoon, but still Norma's heart felt heavy within her. Trevor seemed to sense it. "I hope little Tommy isn't giving you too much trouble," he said.

"Well..." Norma paused, wanting to tell Trevor that his little brother was well behaved, but that would be an outright lie. "He's certainly... never boring," she managed.

Trevor laughed. "Has he drawn all over the blackboard yet?"

"*Nee*, but he did tape Tabitha Petersheim's *kapp* strings to the back of her chair," said Norma.

"Sounds like Tommy." Trevor shook his head. "He's pretty naughty. If it gives you any hope, he'll grow out of it. When I was little, I used to come up with all sorts of mischief."

Norma laughed despite herself. "I hope you haven't taught your little *brudder* any tricks."

"My lips are sealed," said Trevor, winking.

They kept walking, falling into a comfortable silence. Wherever the cloud had come from, it had miraculously gone; maybe the disappointment and frustration over Norma's head had chased it away, but even that was gone now in the face of Trevor's sunny smile. She looked up at him, suddenly ready to be honest. "Trevor, can I ask you something?"

"*Jah*, of course."

"Did you believe everything that my *onkel* told you that day that you came to my *haus*?"

Trevor stopped, staring at her. Norma had to stop and turn to face him.

"Norma, why on earth would I believe him?" he said. "I have eyes, you know. I can see that not a single word he said was even remotely true."

"Really?" Norma's heart flipped over.

"Of course," said Trevor. "Look at that *haus*! I used to play with Abel all the time when we were *kinner*, and I know that the *haus* looks just like it did when your *Mamm* was alive." He looked away, his cheeks brightening. "And I can see how you've cared for your *onkel*. He was talking nonsense, Norma. And I knew it."

Norma started walking again, trembling slightly at the revelation. She hardly dared to believe Trevor's words.

His voice was gentle as he moved to catch up with her. "Have you believed all this time that I thought you were lazy like he said?" he asked. "Is that why you've been avoiding me?"

"I haven't been avoiding you," Norma protested.

Trevor gave her a dubious look.

"All right... maybe a little." Norma sighed. "*Jah*, I did think you believed him."

"I would never believe something like that about you."

Trevor's tone made her blush. She didn't know where to look, so she settled for looking at the sky, her heart barely daring to pray. *Gott, what are You doing?*

"My turn." Trevor smiled. "Can I ask *you* something?"

"*Jah.*"

Trevor paused. She saw a note of nervousness in his eyes as he bit his lip. "Would you..." He cleared his throat. "I mean, do you think you'd like to come on a buggy ride with me this evening?"

This time, it was Norma who stopped. She stared at him, her heart hammering. "Do you mean it?"

"I do." Trevor smiled.

"B-but why?"

"Because..." Trevor tentatively reached out, and his fingers brushed hers, lifting her hands into his. "There's something about you that I've never been able to resist," he whispered. "Even when I was courting Prissy, I knew in my heart that something in you was calling to me. And I know exactly what that something is."

"My apple cobbler?" Norma suggested.

Trevor laughed. "*Nee*, although that certainly calls to my stomach," he said. "It's your heart, Norma. You have been serving your family so wholeheartedly ever since you were a little *maidel*. I admire it. It's a beautiful thing, and I care about you so much for it." Trevor sighed. "I love that I see *Gott* in you. Our Lord shines so brightly in your eyes, and I can't resist Him. At the same time, I see you struggle, and I wish I could help. Please, let me help. Come on that buggy ride with me."

Norma paused, her heart flying back toward home. She thought of Abel, who she knew was suffering with caring for

Silas, and her heart nearly broke. But Trevor's words were still too fresh in the air between them. *I love that I see Gott in you.*

That was when she realized it. Caring for Silas had nothing to do with Silas. She would care for him no matter how crotchety or cruel he could be, because she wasn't caring for him because of anything he had done or anything he was. It was all about who Jesus was, and what He had done. And because that was true, she knew He'd brought this young man across her path for a reason – a reason that not even Silas could defeat.

"Trevor, I would love to go with you tonight," she said simply. "But my family made a big sacrifice for me to be working in the schoolhouse, and I have a duty toward them this evening." She took a deep breath, her confidence wobbling slightly in the face of what she stood to lose. "I have to take care of Silas right now. But when my *dat* and *brudders* get back and the usual teacher is in the school again, then, well, I hope you'll still want to go."

She held her breath for a second as he gazed at her. What was that in his eyes? Regret? Longing? Pity?

Trevor closed his fingers lightly over hers. "Of course. I understand," he said, smiling, his eyes alight. "Would you do me the honor of letting me walk you home, though?"

Norma grinned, her heart thundering. "That would be *wunderlich*," she said. "I'd like that very much."

Trevor held out his arm, and Norma threaded hers through it. They walked side by side through the changing landscape, and with every cell in her body, Norma praised the God Who gave her strength.

The strength to finally see the truth. And the strength to forgive Silas Glick.

Chapter Ten

Norma was surprised to see a lamp burning in the kitchen when she tiptoed down the stairs in her socks. It was just cold enough that she needed to wrap her shawl around herself as she slipped quietly past the sewing room, hearing Silas's deafening snores, and peered around the frame into the kitchen.

"*Daed?*" she whispered.

Daed looked up from where he was sitting at the kitchen table. A Bible lay open in front of him, and he was wearing his square glasses. "Hello, *liebchen*," he said. "Why are you up so late?"

"I just needed some water." Norma sat down next to him and leaned her head on his shoulder. He smelled so familiar. She let out a long sigh. "I'm glad you're home, *Daed*."

"It was a long day, but it's *gut* to be home," said *Daed*. He kissed the side of her head.

Norma glanced over the Bible. "This is *Mamm*'s," she said, startled.

"*Jah*." *Daed* ran a hand over the pages. The text was in High German, but the little annotations in pencil were Pennsylvania Dutch in *Mamm*'s neat copperplate. "I like to take it out whenever I feel a little lost. Sometimes, reading your *mudder*'s insights into *Gott*'s Word makes me feel closer to her – and to Him."

Norma looked up at him. "I had no idea," she said softly.

Daed gave her a squeeze. "I miss your *mudder* as much as you do," he said. "Especially after a day like this."

"Dealing with Silas can be exhausting," Norma agreed.

"That it can, daughter. My older *brudder* has never been kind to me, but I'm so proud of you that it hasn't stopped you from being kind to him." *Daed* smiled at her. "I'm pleased with everything you do, Norma." His voice grew quiet. "And *Mamm* would be, too."

Tears sprang to Norma's eyes. She snuggled closer against her father, feeling something open up in her heart as if she'd been waiting to hear those words all her life. "*Danke, Daed*."

"*Danke* to you," said *Daed*. "Silas has been cruel to you, but you've still taken excellent care of him. I appreciate you, Norma. I should probably say that more often."

"You don't have to," said Norma honestly. She leaned against him, and a few moments passed in comfortable silence before she spoke again. "*Daed*, Trevor asked me to go on a buggy ride with him."

"Trevor Schwartz?" *Daed* looked at her in surprise. "Haven't you been sweet on him for months?"

"You knew?"

"I might not be your *mamm*, but I have some intuition," said *Daed* with a smile. "I'm glad for you, Norma."

"Would it be all right if I went with him?" Norma asked. "I feel bad leaving Silas to you all."

"It'll only be for a few hours. We can handle him, and besides, Sheba is running around on two legs again now," *Daed* pointed out. "Of course, you can go, Norma. You didn't need to ask, you know. Most *maidels* wouldn't have. You can go with my blessing."

Norma snuggled closer to him. "You're the blessing."

Daed hugged her tightly. "I don't know if your *Mamm* can see this right now, or if she's so busy beholding the face of our beloved Christ that she doesn't have time for small earthly things," he said softly. "But if she is watching, then I know that she would be happy with how we'd done without her."

"She'd be happy with you, *Daed*," said Norma.

Daed couldn't speak. But the way that he hugged her said everything she needed to hear.

"Ready?"

Norma looked up at Trevor, her heart fluttering in her chest. She couldn't believe that somehow, God had brought her to this very moment. He was smiling as he extended a hand to her, the last of the golden evening light touching his face, lighting up his freckles.

"*Jah*," she whispered. "I'm ready."

She took his hand and allowed him to help her up onto the driver's seat beside him. It was sparkling clean, as was the rest of the buggy; she could see that the reins and harness were freshly oiled, every surface polished. He drove a matching pair of bright bays, and their coats gleamed in the sun, their manes and tails floating with hours of washing and combing.

"They look fast," Norma said nervously.

"They'll only go as fast as you want," said Trevor, and the depth in his eyes spoke about more than the horses.

Norma relaxed. She scooted a little bit closer to him on the seat. "Where are we going to go?" she asked.

"To all the most beautiful places I know," Trevor told her.

Norma smiled. "I think nowhere is more beautiful than right here."

Trevor laughed. "Then let me prove you wrong." He touched the horses' haunches with the reins. "Let's go, beauties."

The horses launched into a brisk trot, and the buggy hummed along on the road. The breeze ran its fingers into Norma's *kapp*, touching her hair, and Trevor laughed, and she laughed. And when they reached the top of the hill and the whole of their community was thrown open before them like a tapestry in the fingers of God, Norma realized how far she could see. All the way across the town. All the way to the bluish horizon.

All the way into the future God had intended for her.

Chapter Eleven

Silas was dying. Norma knew he had been dying for a long time, but right now she could almost feel each of the minutes of his life peeling away from him, fluttering off into the shadows like petals pulled from a rose. She pulled the covers up over his shoulders and tucked them around his body, moving gently where she knew all his old bones ached. He grimaced but didn't seem to have the strength to complain anymore. His face was ashen, pinched where once it had been so spread out and flabby, and it seemed that every day added a new line around his mouth and eyes.

"Are you warm enough, *Onkel?*" asked Norma gently.

"Warm enough? How can I be warm enough in this drafty place?" Silas grumbled. "And with hardly any quilts to cover me. It's awful, I tell you. I can't believe I haven't caught my death yet."

Norma touched his shoulder. "Do you need an extra quilt?"

Silas sighed. It seemed as though the fight had gone out of him, and he looked away. "*Nee.* It's all right."

"All right." Norma smoothed out the quilt around him and adjusted his pillows slightly. It had been more than a week since Silas had been able to get out of bed, but she had checked him carefully for bed sores, and he didn't have any yet. The visiting nurse had left her a tube of cream for them just in case.

Silas cleared his throat. Norma waited, ready for another tirade, but instead his voice sounded old and tired. "Is there any more of that pain medicine?"

Norma knelt beside the bed, laying a hand on her *onkel's* chest. "I'm sorry, Silas. I've given you everything that I can. You can have some more in four hours."

"Don't see what the point is in holding back," Silas grumbled. "I'm dying in any case." He coughed. "Never mind. I'll just endure it until then."

"I'm sorry," said Norma. "Is there anything else you need?"

Silas shook his head, and Norma rose to her feet. "I'll let you get some rest, then."

"Wait."

Surprised, Norma watched as Silas wriggled a skeletal hand out from under the covers. He held it out to her and gazed up, his watery eyes hollow. "Stay a minute."

"Of course." Norma reached toward his hand, a little surprised when his bony fingers folded around hers. She pulled the wooden chair by the bed a little closer and settled into it. "What can I do for you?" She touched the Bible on the nightstand. "Can I read to you?"

Silas studied the book for a few moments. "I haven't taken much of that book to heart lately," he said softly.

"Better late than never," said Norma, smiling.

"Don't you make fun of me, you cheeky young upstart," snapped Silas. Then, he relented. "*Jah*, do that."

Norma took the book down and looked for a happy chapter to read. As her fingers were running down the pages, Silas spoke again. "I never married, you know."

Norma looked up at him. It was the first time he'd spoken to her for anything but demands or complaints, and she was surprised, even though she knew he'd never married. "Why was that?" she asked, trying to make conversation.

"It didn't seem like it was for me." Silas picked at a loose thread on the quilt, not looking at her. "I thought your *vadder* was a fool to marry that *maidel* and have so many *kinner* with so little money. I told him as much, too. Over and over, especially with each new *boppli* being born."

Sounds like you, Norma thought, but she didn't say it. Silas sighed. "But now, I don't know who was the wise one," he said softly.

The silence grew heavy and awkward. Norma picked a random psalm and began to read. "Oh, that men would praise the Lord for His goodness," she began, "for His wonderful..."

"Norma," said Silas, sharply.

Norma looked up at him, expecting a complaint. "*Jah?*"

Silas gripped her arm with surprising strength despite the bones that stood out in his hand. His eyes were fierce. "If you ever get the chance, you get married, do you hear?" he said.

Norma blinked at him. "All – all right," she stammered.

"*Gut.*" Silas relaxed back onto the pillows, closing his eyes. "You can read now."

Norma stared at him for a few more seconds, her heart strangely touched. Had he really been caring about her, somewhere deep below all that complaining, all this time?

"Well, what are you waiting for?" Silas snapped.

But his words lacked their old vehemence. Norma began to read, a strange feeling of reconciliation filling her heart.

"Fall doesn't get any more perfect than this," Norma said,

gazing at the blazing foliage on either side of the footpath. Her feet crunched musically on the fallen leaves that piled on either side of them, transforming the world into a frozen study of flame. Everything seemed to be made of gold: the shining leaves, the corn in the fields just beyond the trees, the lighting, the motes of dust dancing in the sunshine with every step she took. The feeling in her heart.

"*Nee*, it doesn't," Trevor agreed, but he wasn't looking around at the landscape. He was looking down at her.

"It's almost Thanksgiving," Norma commented. She sighed. "I hope I'll be able to bake something for the family gathering."

"Me too," said Trevor. "*Danke* for coming on this walk with me. I know you're busy."

"*Daed* gave me a quick break." Norma smiled. "We just have to be back in half an hour, that's all."

"I'd better make this quick, then." Trevor stopped and gripped both of her hands, turning her to face him. Her heart seemed to take flight when she saw the look in his eyes; delighted, hopeful, and just a little mischievous.

In one awkward movement, Trevor bit his lower lip and squeezed her hands. "Norma Glick," he said formally. "I had a very long speech planned, but you're in a hurry, and honestly, I can't remember any of it now that I'm looking into your eyes. I just know that you are the woman *Gott* made for my heart, and that I love you and want to love you for the rest of my life." He took a deep breath. "Will you marry me?"

Norma wanted to squeal, or dance, or maybe sprout wings and leap into the sky and turn a loop-the-loop. Instead, she just clapped both hands over her mouth and burst into tears.

"Norma?" Trevor sounded terrified.

"*Jah!*" Norma threw her arms around his neck. "Over and over, *jah!*"

"*Gut.*" Trevor laughed in relief, hugging her back. "But why are you crying?"

"Because I'm happy." Norma leaned back against the bark of a tree, mopping inelegantly at her eyes. "But also because, Trevor, we have to wait. I can't leave my family now with Silas. We need to wait until... until he passes." She paused. "I don't know how long that's going to be."

Trevor leaned forward and pressed his lips to her forehead, a touch as gentle as a falling leaf kissing the earth.

"I'll wait a thousand years for you," he whispered.

Chapter Twelve

It didn't take a thousand years. It was only a couple of weeks later when Dinah was sitting at the kitchen table, working on her wedding dress. "How about a dark green?" she suggested.

Norma pursed her lips as she scrubbed at the dishes, thinking about it. "Don't you think it's a little... well, inappropriate?" she suggested.

"We're not Old Order, you know," said Dinah, laughing. "I think it's all right. Esther Dienner wore dark green to church the other day."

"I like green. It's the same color as Trevor's eyes," said Norma. "But how about navy?"

"Navy could work, too. It's more traditional," said Dinah. She shook the dark blue fabric of the dress she was working on. "But then I'll tell everyone you stole my idea."

Norma laughed. "Amish have been getting married wearing blue for centuries, Dinah," she said. "I think *you* stole the idea first."

Dinah laughed. "That is true." She grinned at Norma. "It's so *gut* to see you so happy, my friend. Trevor is *gut* for you."

"*Gott* is *gut* to me," said Norma. "He has given me the future I was sure I couldn't have. I can hardly believe His mercy and grace."

"His power is amazing," Dinah agreed. She giggled. "Soon our *kinner* are going to be playing on the lawn together."

Norma loved the idea. "All right, but I'm going to have *kinner* first."

"The race is on," said Dinah, laughing.

"Norma!"

This time, the yell from the sewing room made Norma's heart stand still. It was weak and desperate, more of a yelp than a roar. She ran to the sewing room, Dinah hot on her heels, without bothering to dry her soapy hands. Silas was half sitting up, his face ash gray. The bed was covered in a great splash of blood, and more blood dribbled from his lower lip.

Norma heard Dinah gasp sharply behind her. Her own blood was rushing in her ears, but she knew that she had to stay calm. "Run to the Bontragers," she said. "They have a telephone shed. Call 911."

"I'm going," said Dinah, grabbing her skirts and bolting out of the house.

Norma hurried to Silas's side and pulled away the blood-soaked sheets. He clutched at her hand, panting, his eyes wide.

"It's all right, Silas," she told him. "Help is coming. *Gott* is with you."

"Where is my *brudder*?" Silas asked.

"*Daed* and the boys went to deliver hay at the Fisher farm. We'll get in touch with them as soon as we can," said Norma. "And Sheba is at school."

Silas nodded. "*Gut*," he said quietly. "I don't want them to see this."

Then he heaved, and Norma rolled him over to vomit up another great bout of blood onto the floor. She stroked his back, murmuring words of encouragement scary long minutes before sirens howled in the distance, shattering the peace of the Amish countryside. In minutes, two *Englisch* men in their uniforms and clonking boots came into the house, dragging a gurney, stethoscopes swinging around their necks.

"Hello," said one of them, unfazed by the pool of blood on the floor. "What's the trouble?"

"He has colon cancer," Norma told them. "He's seventy-five."

"Okay." The taller man, with "Paramedic" on his uniform, went to examine Silas. Norma got out of his way. She looked at the shorter man, the one whose uniform said "EMT".

Norma hovered as the two men gently scooped Silas up into the gurney and hurried out toward the ambulance, a flashing imposition of growling diesel and flashing lights on the lawn of her home. Norma paused to slam the door behind her and ran out to the ambulance just as they were sliding the gurney up inside.

"I want her to come with me. Let her come with me," Silas was croaking, his lips flecked with blood.

"Of course, she can come with you," said the EMT soothingly as the paramedic was slipping a needle into Silas's arm, tucking an oxygen mask over his face.

"Let's get going," the paramedic said, his voice strained.

Dinah had returned, racing into the yard. "I'll tell your *dat*!" she hollered.

Norma scrambled up into the ambulance, and the EMT shut the door behind her. In a few minutes, the vehicle lurched queasily, and Norma felt it bump across the drive. The feeling was alien, but she didn't have time to worry about it. She grabbed Silas's hand and hung on tightly as the paramedic continued to work on Silas. The old man wasn't talking now, and his eyes were slightly glazed, but they were fixed firmly on

Norma. She hummed a hymn to him, stroking his hand gently.

"Mike, you've gotta give me some diesel, man," the paramedic said sharply, glancing up at a monitor screen. "He's peri-arrest."

"We're nearly there. Half a block," the EMT called back.

Silas struggled to say something. Norma leaned closer. "What is it, *Onkel?*" she asked, worried.

Silas wheezed out a word, but Norma couldn't hear it over the hissing oxygen mask. With a compassionate glance, the paramedic leaned over and slipped the mask off for a moment.

"Marry," Silas was croaking. "Marry."

"What?" Norma leaned a little closer.

"Marry that boy," Silas wheezed.

The paramedic replaced the mask, but the old man's eyes were closing. A continuous beep turned into a long, electric wail, and the paramedic looked up at her.

"I'm sorry," he said softly, reaching up to turn off the monitor. "We're losing him."

The paramedic reached over to rest a hand on her arm. "There's nothing anyone could have done," he said quietly.

"I know," said Norma. She looked down at her *onkel*, felt his fingers loosen in hers. To her surprise, she wasn't ready to let go of his hand. Her chest felt like it was being squeezed, and she leaned over, pulling the oxygen mask gently off Silas's face so that she could press her lips for the first and last time to his blood-smeared forehead. "*Gut*-bye, *Onkel*," she whispered in Pennsylvania Dutch. "*Danke* for everything that you taught me."

The EMT opened the back door once they'd arrived at the hospital, and she climbed out of the ambulance as a team of doctors hurried out, the paramedic shaking his head. Standing in the parking lot, she wrapped her arms around herself, not knowing what to feel. Fear, sorrow, hope, excitement – it all clashed in her heart much too loudly.

So she sat down by a nearby wall. And for quite a while, she cried for Silas Glick.

The weather seemed to be so ridiculously cheerful for a funeral. Norma felt as though there should be gray clouds as she gripped her father's hand tightly. They were the last two people left by the graveside; the other members of their community had offered their condolences and left to go back for the large meal.

Daed's eyes were wet as he gazed down at the fresh, red earth. "I almost didn't expect to be this sad," he said softly. "Silas and I never got along."

"Neither did we," Norma agreed. She squeezed *Daed*'s fingers. "He asked about you right before he died, you know."

Daed looked up, his eyes filled with guilt. "I should have been there."

"*Nee*." Norma shook her head. "He said he was glad you weren't there to see him that way. He was protecting you."

"I think he protected me from more than I realize," said *Daed* softly. He gave the simple headstone one final glance. "I tried so hard to connect with him."

"Maybe you did connect with him, *Daed*," said Norma softly. "He just never let you know it."

"Maybe." *Daed* sighed. "But I know it was his time to go." He looked at Norma. "In a way, I'm sorry you needed to do so much for him."

"Don't be." Norma paused. "Silas showed me that being needed is exhausting sometimes, but it's a *gut* thing. We all need to be needed."

Daed squeezed her hand. "Someone with a heart like yours will always be needed."

He turned, and Norma followed him away from the grave, heading toward where their buggy stood at the top of the road with Snowy drooping patiently in his harness. *Daed* looked up at her, his eyes still damp. "Now you can have that future you deserve," he murmured.

"What do you mean?" asked Norma.

Daed pointed. Norma followed the direction of his finger to the end of the lane, where Trevor was standing a respectful distance away, his hands tucked into his coat against the growing cold. Her heart flipped over, and she felt pulled toward him as if by a giant magnet.

Daed let go of her hand and smiled at her. "It's time to live the life *Gott* has planned for you," he whispered.

"Can I?" she murmured.

"Of course." *Daed* nodded. "Go."

Norma went. She went as fast as she could, her feet traipsing over the cold earth, her arms held out. And when Trevor caught her, and spun her around, she could feel a change of seasons more dramatically than the blazing fall colors all around her.

Her father was right. It was time to live the next part of the life *Gott* had planned for her.

The End

Continue Reading...

✣

Thank you for reading **Amish Caretaker! Are you wondering what to read next?** Why not read **Sweet Forgiveness?** Here's a **peek for you:**

Guilt could make a man do things he'd swore he'd never do.

Jeremy Slagel had promised himself he'd never return to Baker's Corner, Indiana. Yet, here he was. And none too happy about it either.

He pulled open the door of the dry goods store, a cheery bell jingling in jarring contrast to his current mood. He stepped inside.

"Jeremy?" the shop owner greeted him in a loud voice, an expression of surprised recognition crossing his lined face. "It must be about five years since the last time I saw you in here. What brings you back to town?"

"I'm taking care of the family farm now that my *daed* has become too sick to handle the chores any longer."

Jacob gave Jeremy an approving nod. "It's *gut* that you're back."

Jeremy made a noncommittal sound in response. Unfortunately, he couldn't agree with the older man's sentiment. This was the very last place in the world he wanted to be.

Growing up, he couldn't wait to leave, and he'd hightailed it out of Baker's Corner at the first opportunity—the same way his four older brothers had left before him. Now he was back. The only one of the five Slagel boys who had felt compelled to return.

His conscience had a lot to answer for. Especially given the fact that his feelings for this place—and for one man in particular—were entirely justified.

He ignored the knowledge that not everything about Baker's Corner had been unbearable, but things had been bad enough. And that came down to just one reason—Jeremy's *daed*.

After all the misery he'd wrought throughout Jeremy's boyhood, Isaiah Slagel didn't deserve consideration from his youngest son now. But even knowing that, Jeremy hadn't been able to ignore the bishop's summons when he called Jeremy back home.

Nee, not home, he thought. This place wasn't home. Not anymore. It hadn't been for a long time. He lived in Illinois now. His life was there, and he intended to return to his farm just as soon as he was able.

Jeremy felt a sharp pang of shame at the relief the thought brought, since his eventual escape hinged on a man's death. His *daed's* death. After the older man was gone, Jeremy's duty here would be done.

He felt guilty for that thought, too.

Caring for a family member shouldn't be an unwanted obligation. But Isaiah Slagel had never been an easy man to love.

VISIT HERE To Read More:

http://www.ticahousepublishing.com/amish-miller.html

Thank you for Reading

If you **love Amish Romance**, **Visit Here**

https://amish.subscribemenow.com/

to find out about all **New Hannah Miller Amish Romance Releases! We will let you know as soon as they become available!**

If you enjoyed *Amish Caretaker!* would you kindly take a couple minutes to leave a positive review on Amazon? It only takes a moment, and positive reviews truly make a difference. I would be so grateful! Thank you!

Turn the page to discover more Hannah Miller Amish Romances just for you!

More Amish Romance from Hannah Miller

Visit HERE for Hannah Miller's Amish Romance

https://ticahousepublishing.com/amish-miller.html

About the Author

Hannah Miller has been writing Amish Romance for the past seven years. Long intrigued by the Amish way of life, Hannah has traveled the United States, visiting different Amish communities. She treasures her Amish friends and enjoys visiting with them. Hannah makes her home in Indiana, along with her husband, Robert. Together, they have three children and seven grandchildren. Hannah loves to ride bikes in the sunshine. And if it's warm enough for a picnic, you'll find her under the nearest tree!